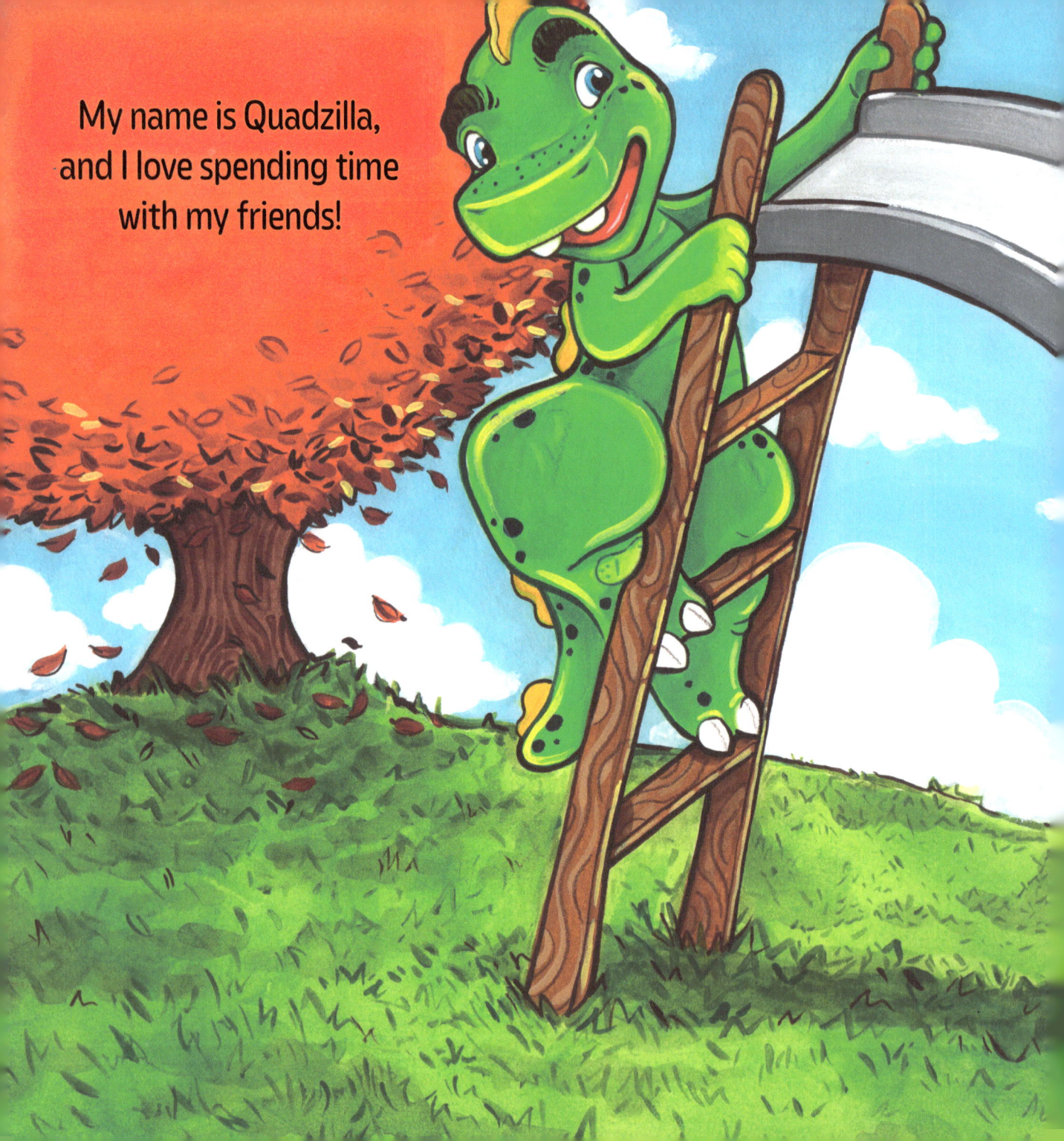

Robirda loves to ride her new bike.

When she lets me try, I fall down and can't reach the pedals.

Teeny is so small,
he's great at hide and seek!

Whenever we play that game,
I'm the first one found.

My friend Bubs is the best at swimming!

But my hands and feet aren't as helpful as hers.

No one plays the piano better than my friend, Spike!

There's no way I could play as fast as he does...

Even though I like spending time with my friends, sometimes it makes me sad.

They all know what they're good at, but I haven't found where I fit.

Then Wooly says, "We want to try a new game!"
"Play for a little while," says Teeny. "Maybe you'll like it!"
Even though I'm nervous, I decide to give it a try.

Together, we go outside and play football.

Robirda can kick the ball farther than anyone!

Teeny is so good at dodging, no one can catch him.

Bubs always catches the ball!

Wooly can see across the field, so he knows just where to pass.

When he passes the ball to me, I get scared.

What if I'm not good at football?

But then I catch it! I run and run and run…

My friends are so happy for me, and I am proud of myself.

When the game started, I was nervous,
but I'm glad I kept trying to play!

Now I know that it's fun to keep trying...even if it isn't easy right away.

Robirda asks, "Do you want to play football again tomorrow?"

"Yes!" I cheer. "I love playing football, but there's something else I love too..."

Published by Orange Hat Publishing 2023

ISBN 9781645387145 | Hardcover
ISBN 9781645385691 | Paperback

Quadzilla Finds His Footing
Written by AJ Dillon
Illustrated by Summer Morrison
Copyrighted © 2023 by AJ Dillon
All Rights Reserved

For bulk orders and wholesale information,
please contact the publisher:
shannon@orangehatpublishing.com | 414-212-5477

This publication and all contents within may not
be reproduced or transmitted in any part or in
its entirety without the written permission of the
author and publisher.

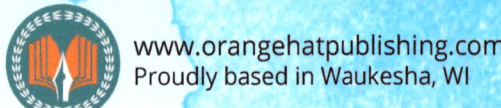

www.orangehatpublishing.com
Proudly based in Waukesha, WI

Trey,
we hope you find your footing.

Love,
Mom and Dad

Printed in the USA
CPSIA information can be obtained
at www.ICGtesting.com
JSHW041218241023
50732JS00001B/1